# Birthdays Around the World

Written by
**Margriet Ruurs**

Illustrated by
**Ashley Barron**

**Kids Can Press**

Happy Birthday to Nico and Aidan — M.R.

To my mom, for making my childhood birthday parties so magical — A.B.

Acknowledgments

This book would not have been possible without the help of real children around the world.
Many thanks to them and to others who provided information and help:

Canada: Michael and Geraldine Kusugak
U.S.A.: Tammy Yee, Leslie Hayashi
Jamaica: Judy Vizbar
Peru: Mercedes Romero
Latvia: Anita Walters, Ieva Dravina
Russia: Angela Lebedeva
Belgium: Remco van Mourik, Karen Van Brussel, Vincent van der Heijden
Ghana: Sylvia Ampofo, Enyo Harlley
Lesotho: Nthabeleng Lephoto
India: Ninoshka DSilva
Japan: Shinobu Murata
Cambodia: Im Chhourn, Chhit Srey Peov, Anne Mackie
Vietnam: Phạm Phú Dũng, Andrew Lam
Australia: Dana Menghetti

Text © 2017 Margriet Ruurs
Illustrations © 2017 Ashley Barron

All rights reserved. No part of this publication may be reproduced, stored in a retrieval
system or transmitted, in any form or by any means, without the prior written permission
of Kids Can Press Ltd. or, in case of photocopying or other reprographic copying, a license from
The Canadian Copyright Licensing Agency (Access Copyright). For an Access Copyright license, visit
www.accesscopyright.ca or call toll free to 1-800-893-5777.

Kids Can Press gratefully acknowledges the financial support of the Government
of Ontario, through the Ontario Media Development Corporation; the Ontario Arts Council;
the Canada Council for the Arts; and the Government of Canada, through the CBF,
for our publishing activity.

Published in Canada and the U.S. by Kids Can Press Ltd.
25 Dockside Drive, Toronto, ON  M5A 0B5

Kids Can Press is a Corus Entertainment Inc. company

www.kidscanpress.com

The artwork in this book was rendered in cut-paper collage and Photoshop.
The text is set in Chapparal Display.

Edited by Katie Scott
Designed by Marie Bartholomew

Printed and bound in Shenzhen, China, in 3/2017 by C&C Offset

CM 17 0 9 8 7 6 5 4 3 2 1

**Library and Archives Canada Cataloguing in Publication**

Ruurs, Margriet, 1952–, author
Birthdays around the world / written by Margriet Ruurs ;
illustrated by Ashley Barron.

(Around the world)
ISBN 978-1-77138-624-1 (hardback)

1. Birthdays — Juvenile literature. I. Barron, Ashley, illustrator II. Title.

GT2430.R88 2017      j394.2      C2016-906423-9

# Contents

# Birthdays Around the World

Everybody in the world has a birthday. But birthdays are not celebrated in the same way everywhere.

Some people have big parties, with special food, gifts and a birthday song. For others, it's more important to offer thanks or to give small presents to others. Some people don't celebrate their birthdays at all, or don't even know when they were born.

Sometimes a person's very first birthday is the most important. And some children celebrate their third, fifth or seventh birthdays during a special ceremony.

Let's have a look at how children all around the world celebrate their birthdays. Maybe they celebrate just like you do!

# Meet these children from around the world.

**Bram**
Belgium

**Arvaarluk**
Canada

Hawaii, U.S.A.

**Alana & Kainoa**
U.S.A.

**Opal & Delroy**
Jamaica

**Mercedes**
Peru

**Maame**
Ghana

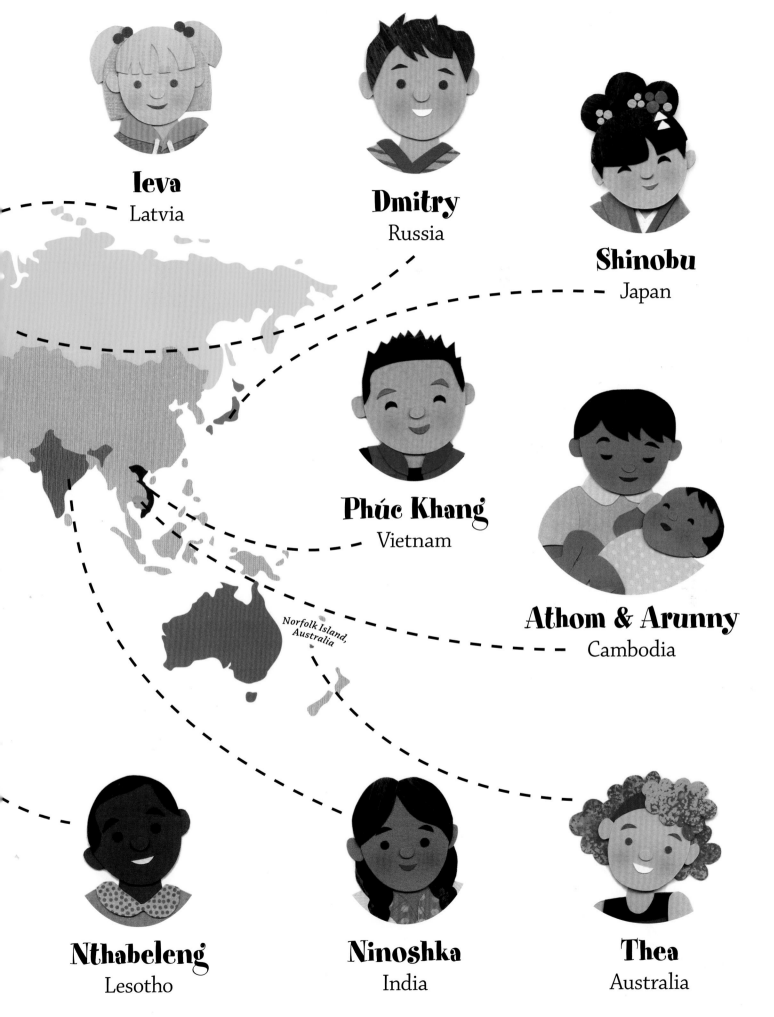

**Ieva**
Latvia

**Dmitry**
Russia

**Shinobu**
Japan

**Phúc Khang**
Vietnam

**Athom & Arunny**
Cambodia

Norfolk Island,
Australia

**Nthabeleng**
Lesotho

**Ninoshka**
India

**Thea**
Australia

# Arvaarluk lives in Nunavut, Canada.

*Quvianaq inuulauravit!*

I celebrate my birthday like many kids in Canada. My friends come over for a party at my house. There are balloons and party hats, and we play games and eat hot dogs and cake.

Everyone sings "Happy Birthday," and I make a wish before blowing out the candles on my cake. Then I open the gifts that people brought.

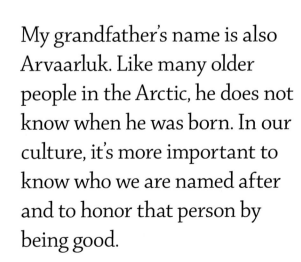

My grandfather's name is also Arvaarluk. Like many older people in the Arctic, he does not know when he was born. In our culture, it's more important to know who we are named after and to honor that person by being good.

# Alana and Kainoa live in Hawaii, U.S.A.

*Hau`oli lā hānau!*

Today my baby brother, Kainoa, turns one! First birthdays are a big celebration in Hawaii. We have a party called a luau, and all of our relatives come.

Kainoa is wearing his *palaka* aloha shirt, and I am wearing a lei. We watch a Chinese Lion dance and have our faces painted.

Later, we have a yummy feast with purple *poi*, *lau lau*, *lomi lomi* salmon, long rice and roasted *kālua* pig. But my favorite dish is *haupia*, a custard dessert made from coconut milk.

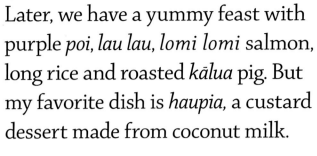

Listen! Our friend is playing his ukulele. Everyone is dancing, and my *tūtū* is teaching me hula!

# Opal and Delroy live in Kingston, Jamaica.

*Shhh* ... Delroy is coming!
Today is his birthday, and I am hiding
behind the breadfruit tree that
was planted for him on
the day he was born.

I jump out and dump flour all over Delroy.
It is my favorite birthday tradition!
He roars with laughter, and we wrestle
in the grass.

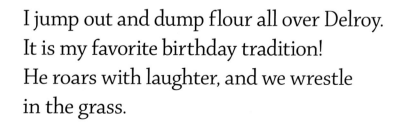

When Delroy's friends and the rest of our family get here, we all sing "Happy Birthday, Everyone!" Then we eat ackee and saltfish, jerk chicken and rice 'n peas. And Delroy's favorite dessert: chocolate cake!

Our father pretends to bring water for the tree. But in his bucket is more flour that he dumps on Delroy's head! With his white hair, Delroy sure looks older now.

# Mercedes lives in Piura, Peru.

*Feliz cumpleaños!*

Welcome to my party!
Everyone is here —
my friends, family and
neighbors. I sent them
all invitations.

The house is decorated with streamers and balloons.
The table is loaded with cake, *frunas*, *galletas*, popcorn,
jelly and a purple pudding called *mazamorra morada*.

All the kids are wearing party hats.
Some of our guests brought gifts,
like soap, shampoo or clothing. I like
the toys best: a ball and a tea set!

My favorite part is when Papa pulls the cord on the
piñata, and candies and toys rain down on our heads!
When it's time for my friends to go home,
I give them *sorpresas* and balloons.

# Ieva lives in Kuldiga, Latvia.

*Daudz laimes dzimšanas dienā!*

Mmm! I can smell the *kliņģeris* baking in the oven. Mom is making this sweet bread especially for my birthday.

My friends and relatives come over. They bring flowers, always bunched in odd numbers, like nine, eleven or thirteen. I also get flowers on my Name Day, which is just as important as my birthday. December 24 is the day for my name — Ieva.

When the *kliņģeris* is ready, everyone sings the birthday song, and I blow out the candles. The smoke sends my birthday wish straight up to God.

Then I get to sit on the birthday chair!
I am raised high up in the air.
One ... two ... three ... four ... five ... six ... seven!
One bump for each year of my life!

# Dmitry lives in Chelyabinsk, Russia.

*S dn'em rozhdeniya!*

Today is the best day of the year! On my birthday, I get to treat my class to delicious pies and cookies, fizzy drinks and lemonade.

After school, my friends come to our house.
We've decorated it with balloons and signs.
We blow bubbles, and a cheerful clown
performs for us.

Then we eat wonderful treats like
*blini* with caviar, and dumplings
filled with meat and mushrooms.

Everyone sings the traditional birthday song about
being happy even on a rainy day. The boy in the song
is sad that birthdays come only once a year.
And so am I!

# Bram lives in Ghent, Belgium.

*Gelukkige verjaardag!*

When I wake up, my family marches into my bedroom, banging pots and pans, and carrying gifts. They are singing *"Lang Zal Hij Leven"* — our birthday song that wishes me a long life!

At school, I treat everyone in my class to candies. The whole class sings for me, too, and I wear a paper crown all day.

Many relatives come to our house after school.
My aunts and uncles who can't visit mail me a birthday
card or send a text message. For dinner, I get to choose
my favorite food: fries with applesauce!

We have a cake with candles,
one for each year. I blow them out
in one big breath so that my wish
will come true.

# Maame lives in Accra, Ghana.

*Awo-da!*

First thing this morning, my mother cooks *oto*, especially for me. She mashes yams with palm oil and boils the eggs. The smell makes my mouth water!

All day long, people are extra nice to me. My father gives me a soft drink, and I get a few coins from my auntie.

My friends and I play *ampe*,
our favorite game. It takes skill
and practice to jump and clap
and score points.

Tonight, we will all eat our dinner of *jollof*
and fried plantains, with a special piece of
chicken just for me!

# Nthabeleng lives in Mokhotlong, Lesotho.

*Letsatsi le monate la tsoalo!*

I am not sure when my birthday is.
But on July 17, our entire country celebrates
the birthday of our beloved King!

Each part of the country holds its own celebration.
The King attends one every year, and this year, he is
coming to Mokhotlong! The party starts the day before
with dancing, singing and traditional pony races.

The next day, there is a royal gun salute and a military parade. Large crowds of people, many wearing traditional blankets and *seshoeshoe* dresses, come to watch.

We all sing our national anthem and cheer, "Hip, hip, hooray for our King!"

# Ninoshka lives in Koipur, India.

*Janam din mubarak!*

Today, I turn six years old! Early in the morning, we perform *puja* — a ceremony for the Hindu gods.

The smell of sandalwood fills the air. My mother asks for a blessing and arranges a tray to give thanks, with flowers for beauty, milk for peace, rice for a long life and honey for kindness.

The priest will come to read my Kundali,
the record of my life's most important events.
It also predicts my future based on the day
and time I was born.

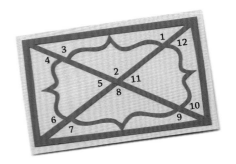

After the ceremony, I bring sweets and chocolates
to school to share with all my friends!

# Shinobu lives in Toyohashi, Japan.

*O tanjoubi omedetou!*

My birthday was in August, but on November 15, I celebrate Shichi-Go-San. This special day is for children who turn three, five or seven this year.
We give thanks for growing older, stronger and healthier.

It will take hours for my mother to help me dress in a silk kimono and do my hair.

Then my family and I go to the temple.
The monk blesses me, prays for me
and gives me a bag of candies called
Chitose Ame. Cranes and turtles on
the bag represent a long life.

After, my grandparents take pictures,
and we eat sushi and *seki han*,
red rice that brings good luck.

# Athom and Arunny live in Phnom Penh, Cambodia.

*Reek reay thngai kamnaet!*

In my country, we don't usually celebrate birthdays. My grandparents don't even know when they were born.

Instead, we celebrate Pro Kok Kun, when a baby turns one month old. Today is the celebration for my new sister. Our parents chose the perfect name for her — Arunny means "morning sun."

Our relatives gather for a party with lots of dancing to welcome the new baby.

Then, a monk blesses Arunny with holy water, and I tie a red cotton string around her wrist to bring her good luck.

31

# Phúc Khang lives in Hoi An, Vietnam.

*Chúc mừng sinh nhật!*

Today, rather than on our real birthdays, everyone in our country turns one year older. Tết Nguyên Đán, or Tết for short, is the New Year in our lunar calendar.

The most exciting part, on the first day of Tết, is when my parents give me *li xi*, or lucky money, in a red envelope. It's how children are congratulated for becoming a year older.

We celebrate for an entire week! We will visit
my teachers and relatives to wish them well,
have our fortunes told and burn incense at
the temple to honor our ancestors.

# Thea lives on Norfolk Island, Australia.

This morning, my parents and I gather around the radio. We listen for the song they requested just for me and find out who else on the island has a birthday today.

For breakfast, Mum makes fairy bread with butter and colorful sprinkles that we call hundreds and thousands.

Later, we have a big fish fry at the beach, with all our friends and family. There is even a watermelon seed–spitting contest! My cousins and friends can spit far, but I win!

Before everyone goes home, they sing "Happy Birthday" and everyone cheers, "Hip, hip, hooray!"

# Your Birthday

Every day, children around the world have a birthday. If and how they celebrate depends on where they live.

When is your birthday? Do you have a party, like Mercedes in Peru? Or do you perform a special ceremony, like Ninoshka in India?

Do you blow out candles on a cake, like Bram in Belgium? Do you wear special clothing, like Shinobu in Japan?

In some countries, doing something thoughtful for others — like planting trees or treating your class — is an important birthday tradition.

Do you celebrate a special day?
Is it the day you were born?
Or do you celebrate your Name Day,
like Ieva in Latvia, or the King's birthday,
like Nthabeleng in Lesotho?

The best thing we can all celebrate is how interesting different customs and traditions are, all around the world!

# A Note for Parents and Teachers

The information shared in this book is based on interviews with real people from the different countries that are featured. I asked children and adults how they celebrate their birthdays and was amazed to learn about the variety of customs. I hope that reading their stories will inspire you to discuss your family's own traditions with your child or students, helping to grow their understanding of the world around them.

The following activities are aimed at enriching children's reading experience. Use them as they appear here, or tailor them to fit your needs. Even more ideas can be found on my website: www.margrietruurs.com.

## Pinpointing on the Map

Using a globe or atlas, or the map on pages 6–7, show children where they live. Then locate each of the countries mentioned in the book. Ask children if they know someone who lives or was born in another country. Help them find that place on the map.

## Get the Details

Ask children to interview a grown-up from a different country or culture. How did this person celebrate his or her birthday as a child? Was there a birthday song, food, clothing or gifts? Are there any traditions unique to the country or culture? Ask children to write a story or draw a picture based on what they learn.

## Read Closely

There are many similarities among the children in this book. Ask children the following questions to encourage a close reading of the text and illustrations:

- Many children in the book have special food on their birthdays. Ask readers to find three examples. Have they ever tried any of the foods? What is their favorite food?

- Some children in the book give gifts to others, or make a special offering, on their birthdays. Ask children to find an example.

- Some children in the book don't celebrate their birthdays. Ask children to find two examples. What other traditions do they celebrate?

## Send a Card

Bram in Belgium receives a card in the mail on his birthday. Ask children if they know anyone who lives in another country. When is that person's birthday? Have children send the person a birthday card, and see if that person will send a birthday card to the child, too.

## Happy Birthday!

In this book, you will find many ways to say "happy birthday" in different languages. Arvaarluk in Canada would say *quvianaq inuulauravit* (NAL-liu-niq SIUT-SIA-rit), which translates to "it makes me happy that you were born." Ask children to find the different ways to say "happy birthday" in the book. They can use the glossary on page 40 to help them pronounce the words and find out what they mean. See if they know how to say "happy birthday" in any other language.

Have children create a birthday garland decorated with "happy birthday" in different languages. Use the garland to decorate a house or classroom on a child's birthday.

**1.** Using different colored paper, cut out several 2 x 10 in. (5 x 25 cm) strips.

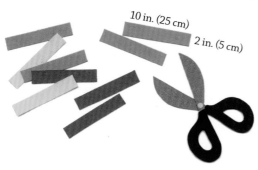

10 in. (25 cm)

2 in. (5 cm)

**2.** On one side, have children write "happy birthday" in another language. On the other side, have them write the English translation.

*Feliz Cumpleaños*

*Happy Birthday*

**3.** Take one strip, and tape the ends together to create a loop.

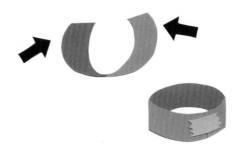

**4.** Show children how to assemble the garland by threading a second strip through the first loop, and taping its ends together. Ask them to continue assembling the garland until they have used up all of the strips.

## Birthday Song

There are many different birthday songs around the world, such as "Happy Birthday, Everyone!" in Jamaica. Ask children to sing the song they know. Then have them learn a birthday song from a different country. Are there any parts of the songs that sound the same? How are they different? For links to videos of birthday songs from around the world, visit www.margrietruurs.com.

# Glossary

Many different writing scripts are used around the world. In this book, the words are written in Latin script, which is what you are reading right now. But in the writing script of Japan, the term "happy birthday" is written like this: お誕生日おめでとうございます. Look for different writing scripts from around the world in the glossary below.

**Pages 8–9: Canada, *Inuktitut***
*Quvianaq inuulauravit* (NAL-liu-niq SIUT-SIA-rit) ᑯᕕᐊᓇᖅ ᐃᓅᓚᐅᕋᕕᑦ: It makes me happy that you were born

**Pages 10–11: U.S.A., *Hawaiian***
*Hauʻoli lā hānau* (how-O-lee LA HA-now): Happy birthday
luau (LOO-ow): Hawaiian feast
*palaka* (PAH-lah-kah): plaid
lei (LAY): flower garland
*poi* (POY): mashed taro root
*lau lau* (LAO lao): pork wrapped in taro leaf
*tūtū* (TOO-TOO): grandmother

**Pages 14–15: Peru, *Spanish***
*Feliz cumpleaños* (fay-LEASE koom-play-AH-nos): Happy birthday
*frunas* (FROO-nas): fruit-flavored candy
*galletas* (gah-YEH-tas): biscuits
*sorpresas* (sore-PRESS-sas): bags with small toys and candies

**Pages 16–17: Latvia, *Latvian***
*Daudz laimes dzimšanas dienā* (DOWDZ LIE-mes DZIM-shun-us DEE-ah-nah): Lots of happiness on your birthday

**Pages 18–19: Russia, *Russian***
*S dnem rozhdeniya* (SDOOM rush-DEE-nyah) С Днём рождения: Happy birthday
*blini* (BLIN-ee): pancake

**Pages 20–21: Belgium, *Flemish***
*Gelukkige verjaardag* (guh-LUCK-eh-guh ver-YAAR-daah): Happy birthday
*"Lang Zal Hij Leven"* (LANG zal hay LAY-ven): "Long Shall He Live"

**Pages 22–23: Ghana, *Ga***
*Awo-da* (ah-WOH-da): Today is your birthday
*jollof* (jo-LOFF): rice dish with tomato and spices

**Pages 24–25: Lesotho, *Sesotho***
*Letsatsi le monate la tsoalo* (le-SAT-see leh mo-nah-tay la TSOH-low): Happy birthday
*seshoeshoe* (SHWAY-shway): printed cotton fabric used for traditional clothing

**Pages 26–27: India, *Hindi***
*Janam din mubarak* (jah-NAM DEEN moo-BAH-rak) जन्म दिन मुबारक: Good wishes on your birthday

**Pages 28–29: Japan, *Japanese***
*O tanjoubi omedetou* (oh TAN-joe-bee oh-MEH-day-toe) お誕生日おめでとうございます: Congratulations on your birthday

**Pages 30–31: Cambodia, *Khmer***
*Reek reay thngai kamnaet* (REEK REE-ay te-NIE KOM-na-uht) រីករាយថ្ងៃខួបកំណើត: Happy birthday

**Pages 32–33: Vietnam, *Vietnamese***
*Chúc mừng sinh nhật* (chook MUNG sing yat): Happy birthday to you